A REAL
CLASS CLOWN

CLASS CLOWN

by Otto Coontz

Little, Brown and Company

BOSTON   TORONTO

Also written and illustrated by Otto Coontz

THE QUIET HOUSE

FIRST EDITION

Library of Congress Cataloging in Publication Data

Coontz, Otto.
  A real class clown.

  SUMMARY: When Rudy the clown attends school
for the first time, he is not appreciated by his
teachers.
  [1. Clowns—Fiction. 2. School stories]
I. Title.
PZ7.C7845Re   [E]   79-13687
ISBN 0-316-15534-9

*Published simultaneously in Canada
by Little, Brown & Company (Canada) Limited*

PRINTED IN THE UNITED STATES OF AMERICA

For Jim Marshall and Shari Rose

Rudy was a born clown. He lived under the Big Top with his parents. The family spent most of their time doing the things that clowns all do: bumping into each other and falling down, pulling the lion by the tail, squirting each other with firehoses, or piling in and out of little cars.

Then one day Rudy's mother told him he had to go to school.

"Why?" asked Rudy. "I want to stay at the circus and make people laugh, like you."

"Everyone has to go to school," his mother told him, "even clowns." She helped him dress and paint his face, and she gave him a cherry for his nose.

Rudy grabbed his lunchbox and called his pet.

"Hurry up, Killer, or I'll be late!" Rudy took Killer's hand, and they started off for school.

"Now, do everything the teacher tells you!" his mother called after him, honking her horn.

When they got to the school, Rudy told Killer to wait outside. Then Rudy stood in the back of the class while the teacher wrote her name.

"This is how to spell it," she said. Then she scraped her fingernails across the board. "And *that* is how it sounds! And now for *your* names!" said Miss Skreech, calling the attendance.

"Here!" shouted Rudy when she called out his name.

11

"What have we here?" asked Miss Skreech, peering over her desk. "You look like you're dressed for the circus!"

"I'm a clown," Rudy answered. Everyone in the classroom laughed — everyone but Miss Skreech.

"Quiet!" she snapped, then peered back down at Rudy.

"That is no way to dress for school! You will have to go home, change your clothes, and take that cherry off your nose!"

Hearing laughter, Killer peeked in the window.

"Aaaargh!" shrieked Miss Skreech.

"Aaaargh!" screamed the class. They all hid under their desks.

"That's just Killer," said Rudy. "He's my pet, and he wouldn't hurt a fly."

"Well, you'll have to get rid of him, too!" snapped Miss Skreech. "School is no place for pets. School is for learning about arithmetic and geography, poetry and science."

Back at the Big Top, Rudy's parents were rehearsing the midget car routine.

"Why aren't you at school?" Rudy's mother called out from the back seat, where she was squashed under all the other clowns.

"Miss Skreech said this was no way to dress for school, and sent me home to change."

"Well, we will just have to ask her how a clown is supposed to dress. Come along, hop on." And they all drove back together.

The little car drove right into the classroom and down the aisle to Miss Skreech's desk.

All the clowns got out. Miss Skreech stepped backward. There were so *many* clowns!

"Now then, Miss Skreech, what is the matter with Rudy's clothes?" asked his mother.

"Rudy cannot dress like that when he comes to school," Miss Skreech replied.

"Why not?" asked Rudy's mother. "Rudy's a born clown! How else should a clown dress?" Miss Skreech had no answer for that, for Rudy *was* a clown.

"But the children will laugh at him!" warned Miss Skreech.

"I should hope so!" replied Rudy's mother. She sent Rudy to his desk and climbed back into the car with the other clowns.

"After all, he wouldn't be much of a clown if they didn't laugh, now would he?" And the little car drove off. The children roared with laughter.

20

"Quiet!" shouted Miss Skreech. "Stop clowning around. This isn't a circus! Everyone open your arithmetic books!" Miss Skreech was not pleased. Rudy was what she had always dreaded: a real Class Clown.

"It's almost as good as the Big Top," Rudy told his mother that night. "They laugh at everything I do. Everyone except Miss Skreech. Now I have to do my homework. Miss Skreech told us to make up a multiplication problem, and I want to ask Eleanor to help."

Rudy went out to the elephant tent and did not come back till bedtime.

The next day, Rudy brought Eleanor and a big pail of peanuts to school.

"Not again!" scolded Miss Skreech. "I've warned you about pets!"

"It's okay," Rudy explained. "Eleanor came to help with my math problem."

"Then get on with it!" frowned Miss Skreech, hoping Eleanor would leave as soon as the problem was solved.

"If Eleanor eats fifty peanuts for breakfast," Rudy explained, counting the peanuts from the pail, "then eats twice that many for lunch," he said, making another pile, "and three times that many for supper, then how many peanuts does Eleanor eat in a day?"

Eleanor inhaled peanuts faster than the class could count them, and Rudy had to count out six more piles before everyone had the answer.

"If she ate any more," said Miss Skreech, "we'd know just how many peanuts it takes to explode an elephant!"

When Rudy got home for supper that night, he had so much to tell he could hardly eat a bite.

"It was wonderful. Everyone laughed at Eleanor. Everyone but Miss Skreech. But she gave me an A in 'creating problems,' and Eleanor got a gold star for leaving the classroom without stepping on anyone."

Rudy's mother was very proud.

"Tomorrow, we each have to do a science project," Rudy told her, "and I'm going to take Peter to help me."

The next day, Rudy came to school carrying a very long, skinny box filled with holes.

"What's in that?" Miss Skreech asked, raising her eyebrows.

"It's my science experiment," Rudy answered.

"Well, let's get it over with," said Miss Skreech, eyeing the box suspiciously.

When Rudy opened the box, Peter stuck just his nose over the edge. Then his tongue flickered.

Miss Skreech screamed very loud and fainted. Snakes are attracted to thumps on the ground, so Peter slithered right up to Miss Skreech and coiled himself around her ankles.

When Miss Skreech came to, she began to squirm. Peter's coils grew tighter.

"Just what do you think you're doing?" she groaned.

"I am showing that wherever the head goes," Rudy told her, "the tail is sure to follow."

Peter demonstrated this very well. When he got up to Miss Skreech's neck, Peter looked her right in the eye and stuck out his tongue.

"Look, he's licking his lips! I think that big snake is hungry!" shouted a very smart little girl.

"Oh, no!" answered Rudy. "He's just being friendly."

Miss Skreech did not want to make friends, so Rudy guided Peter's head back into the box.

"See? Wherever the head goes . . ." and soon the rest of Peter was in the box, too.

At supper that night, Rudy's mother asked how the science experiment went.

"Well," said Rudy, "Miss Skreech said it was more like an experiment in terror, but she gave me an A for effort and a nice big chain with a lock on it for Peter's box." Rudy's mother was very proud.

At home, Miss Skreech had other thoughts. "Each day the class laughs louder. I've got to put an end to this."

Then one day she had her chance. Killer had wandered into the schoolyard, so Rudy was sent to take him back home.

"Class," said Miss Skreech when Rudy had gone, "I want to try a little experiment." She made her voice sound as sweet as she could. "Let's see if we can't turn Rudy's smile upside down."

"That doesn't sound very nice," said one little boy.

"Why would you want to do that?" asked another.

"Because," Miss Skreech answered, *"no* one should smile *all* the time. And if he *does,* it's probably because his mouth got *stuck* that way. And when your mouth gets stuck in one position it must begin to *hurt* after a while. Now, wouldn't you all like to help?"

"Oh yes!" answered the class. "Especially if it *hurts!"*

"Good," said Miss Skreech. "Now I want everyone to promise not to laugh at anything Rudy says or does. And we'll see if we can't help to get that smile off his face."

29

When Rudy returned, the class was taking turns reciting their favorite poems. When Rudy's turn came, just to please Miss Skreech, he picked the only poem he knew that was about teachers. It went like this:

When the teacher turns her back while looking for the chalk,
Chew spitballs, candy, pass some notes, giggle, cough and talk.
And when the teacher leaves the room and says, "Now read
*   that book!"*
Fill her drawer with scrambled eggs and ants and worms and
*   gook.*
If she doesn't laugh at this you'll know she's not amused,
That's the time to raise your hand and ask to be excused.

Miss Skreech made a funny face all through the poem, but she did not laugh. Neither did the class. Rudy was disappointed. Then Miss Skreech said, in her sweet voice, "For being so *good,* I am dismissing class early. And remember, tomorrow is careers day, and each of you must tell me what you want to be when you grow up."

That night at supper, Rudy was very quiet. "How was school today?" asked his mother.

"I guess I'm not much of a clown," Rudy answered. "No one laughed in school today. Not even when I told that poem about teachers that Uncle Bopo used to tell."

"Hmm." His mother scratched her head. "Don't worry. Even clowns have a bad day once in a while."

After Rudy went to bed, his mother took something off an old costume and wrapped it up in a small pink box.

The next morning, Rudy still wasn't feeling very cheerful. He painted his face, being sure his smile turned all the way up, and picked out the biggest cherry he could find to put at the end of his nose. On his way out the door, his mother gave him the small pink box.

"Rudy," she said, "I want you to give this to Miss Skreech."

"What is it?" asked Rudy.

"You'll see."

When Rudy arrived at school, all the children had cherries on their noses.

"Rudy!" the class shouted. "Today is careers day! And guess what *we* want to be?"

"A cherry orchard?" Rudy answered. But before anyone could laugh, Miss Skreech glared at the class to remind them of their promise.

"Rudy," asked Miss Skreech, "what do *you* want to be when you grow up?"

"I'm a born clown," Rudy answered, "and that is what I will always be."

"But wouldn't you like to be a fireman, or a doctor, or a teacher like me?" asked Miss Skreech.

"I'm a clown," answered Rudy, "and it is as important to make people laugh as it is to put out fires, or make people better, or to teach them things. That is what my mother says."

Then Rudy remembered the present. "Oh, Miss Skreech, this is for you," and he brought it up to her desk.

"How thoughtful," said Miss Skreech, wondering if what was inside might crawl or bite or jump out at her. She opened it carefully.

Inside was the prettiest corsage Miss Skreech had ever seen.

"What a pretty flower!" exclaimed Rudy.

Miss Skreech picked up the corsage.

"What's this?" she asked, squeezing the bulb. It was a trick flower, and it was filled with water. It squirted Rudy right in the nose. Miss Skreech was so surprised, she burst right out laughing. She tried to pull the corners of her mouth back down, but every time she looked at Rudy's face, she just laughed harder and harder.

"Is it okay to laugh now?" asked someone in the class. But Miss Skreech could not stop laughing to answer. In fact, she laughed right up to the recess bell.

"My!" said Miss Skreech, when she could finally talk again. "I've never *had* such a good laugh!"

The next day Miss Screech was still smiling when the class came in. When the bell rang, she wrote the day's lessons on the board.